# MY TEACHER for PRESIDENT

by Kay Winters    illustrated by Denise Brunkus

SCHOLASTIC INC.
New York Toronto London Auckland Sydney
Mexico City New Delhi Hong Kong Buenos Aires

To Dr. Richard Creasey, a superintendent who encouraged and valued
the work of the teachers in the Palisades School District
K.W.

. . . and Linda Pratt for vice president!
D.B.

ISBN 0-439-69995-9

12 11 10 9 8 7 6 5 4 3 2 1          4 5 6 7 8 9/0

Printed in Singapore          46

First Scholastic printing, September 2004
Designed by Gloria Cheng

Dear Channel 39,

I saw on TV that elections are coming.

At school we have been learning about the president's job.

My teacher would be just right!

Let me know what you think.

My teacher loves white houses.

She's used to being followed everywhere.

When my teacher walks into a room,

people pay attention.

My teacher goes to lots of meetings.

And she's always signing important papers.

My teacher acts quickly when there's an emergency.

And she says health care is important.

My teacher likes to go on trips.

President Robbins travels through Egypt.

President Robbins enjoys Paris.

President Robbins walks the Great Wall of China.

She deals with the media every day.

My teacher would be good for the country.

She wants to clean up the Earth.

She finds jobs for people.

She is a good listener.

She believes in peace.

Love, Oliver

P.S. Just make sure she doesn't leave before

the end of the year.